Jamie's Class Has Something to Say

A Book About Sharing with Grown-Ups

Afsaneh Moradian

Illustrated by Maria Bogade

free spirit
PUBLISHING®

Free Spirit, Free Spirit Publishing, and associated logos are trademarks and/or registered trademarks of Free Spirit Publishing Inc. A complete listing of our logos and trademarks is available at freespirit.com

Library of Congress Cataloging-in-Publication Data
Names: Moradian, Afsaneh, author. | Bogade, Maria, illustrator.
Title: Jamie's class has something to say : a book about sharing with grown-ups / Afsaneh Moradian ; illustrated by Maria Bogade.
Description: Minneapolis, MN : Free Spirit Publishing Inc., [2022] | Audience: Ages 4–8.
Identifiers: LCCN 2021026620 (print) | LCCN 2021026621 (ebook) | ISBN 9781631985539 (hardcover) | ISBN 9781631985546 (pdf) | ISBN 9781631985553 (epub)
Subjects: CYAC: Interpersonal communication—Fiction. | Family life—Fiction. | Schools—Fiction. | LCGFT: Picture books.
Classification: LCC PZ7.1.M66825 Jc 2022 (print) | LCC PZ7.1.M66825 (ebook) | DDC [E]—dc23
LC record available at https://lccn.loc.gov/2021026620
LC ebook record available at https://lccn.loc.gov/2021026621

Free Spirit Publishing does not have control over or assume responsibility for author or third-party websites and their content.

Reading Level Grade 1–2;
Fountas & Pinnell Guided Reading Level K

Edited by Cassandra Sitzman
Cover and interior design by Shannon Pourciau

10 9 8 7 6 5 4 3 2 1
Printed in China
R18860222

Free Spirit Publishing Inc.
6325 Sandburg Road, Suite 100
Minneapolis, MN 55427-3674
(612) 338-2068
help4kids@freespirit.com
freespirit.com

For my mother

Jamie couldn't wait to go to school. The class was going to spend the morning getting ready for Family Day. Jamie was excited for the guests to see all their hard work that afternoon.

Alicia and Joey were hanging up their jackets as Jamie arrived.

"I like your unicorn, Alicia," said Jamie.

"My mom made me wear it." Alicia frowned. "I don't like unicorns. I'm afraid their horns are going to poke me."

"Do you want to wear my sweater to cover it up?" asked Jamie.

"Thanks, Jamie," Alicia said, and put on the sweater.

As the kids entered the classroom,
Ms. Jones reminded them to finish the
name tags they'd started yesterday.
Jamie's was covered in colorful moons.

"Why didn't you tell your mom that you don't like unicorns?" asked Joey.

"She said I looked cute," Alicia explained. "I wanted to wear my sparkly bunny shirt for Family Day."

"My dad wants me to play soccer, but I want to go to art class with Jamie," Joey added. "Soccer practice and art class are at the same time."

Everyone sat down to work on their name tags. "What are you going to do?" Alicia asked.

"I don't know," Joey looked sad. "I wish I could do both. My dad thinks soccer is more important."

Xavier said, "My uncle thinks boys shouldn't cry. He says I have to be tough."

"That isn't very nice," said Alicia.

Once everyone was finished decorating their name tags, they put them in their cubbies so they'd be ready for Family Day.

"My grannie is always telling me to have good manners, use my knife and fork, and never play with my food. Sometimes I really want to make a tower with my corn and a volcano with my mashed potatoes," Cynthia frowned.

"I wish grown-ups were better at listening to us!
They don't always understand what we like or what
we want," said Alicia. She was so frustrated that she
crumpled her paper.

Jamie was listening to the others and thinking about how Jamie's mommy listened to what Jamie had to say, even when she didn't agree.

Then Jamie had an idea. "Why don't we tell them more about ourselves at Family Day?" asked Jamie, and went to find Ms. Jones.

At circle time, Ms. Jones told the class about Jamie's idea. As a special surprise, they were going to make "This Is Me" posters to share with their visitors that afternoon.

Everyone got to work.

When the posters were done, Ms. Jones helped the kids hang them on the wall. Jamie thought they looked beautiful.

Finally, the visitors arrived. Jamie and the other kids were proud to show off their classroom and their posters.

Jamie's mommy loved Jamie's poster and learned some new things about Jamie too. She asked if Jamie would like a glow-in-the-dark moon in Jamie's bedroom. And she promised to use a flashlight to check for monsters under the bed every night.

Jamie heard Alicia's mom ask, "Alicia, honey, why are you wearing that sweater?"

Alicia looked over at Jamie and took a deep breath. "Mom, I don't like unicorns. I didn't want to wear this."

"I'm so sorry! I had no idea. Let's take this off," Alicia's mom said as she put Alicia's headband away.

Xavier's family was reading his poster. His uncle said, "Xavi, you need to toughen up." Xavier didn't know what to say, but Jamie was by his side.

"Everybody cries sometimes," Jamie said. "Ms. Jones says it's okay to cry when we feel like it."

Xavier's uncle thought for a moment. Then he said, "It's true, everybody cries. I'm sorry I told you not to, Xavi. Can you forgive me?" Xavier smiled and gave his uncle a hug.

Cynthia's grannie read Cynthia's poster. She told Cynthia that she was very creative and that she loved her very much. Cynthia beamed when her grannie asked if she wanted to help cook dinner that night.

When they were leaving, Joey's dad asked Jamie's mommy about Jamie's art class.

Jamie looked around at the kids' happy faces. Jamie was glad the class had a chance to share what they liked and didn't like and that the grown-ups had listened. What a great Family Day!

Tips for Parents, Teachers, and Caregivers

When kids feel heard and respected by the adults in their lives, they also feel confident, safe, and self-assured. Having a few trusted adults to talk to is vital for children's development from early childhood through adolescence.

Also important for children is knowing how to speak up about what they need and what they do and don't like—especially when those things differ from what adults prefer or expect. Being able to express likes, feelings, and needs, and knowing they will be taken seriously, is a crucial skill for building relationships and a strong sense of self.

Here are some strategies and activities you can try in your home or classroom to help children feel heard and respected.

Encourage Sharing Likes and Dislikes

Invite children to share their likes and dislikes as a regular part of circle time or classroom discussions, and model how to do this. For example:

- At snack time: "I am going to say 'no thank you' to the graham crackers because I don't like them. What is your favorite snack? What is a snack you don't like?"

- At playtime: "I don't like when someone uses something I was going to use. I feel angry. When someone takes your toy, you can say, 'I don't like when you take my toy. Let's take turns playing with it.'"

- During class: "I raise my hand when I need something. If it's really urgent and I can't wait, I walk over to my teacher and say what I need."

Ask Children's Opinions

Finding out why children like or don't like something and asking about their interests shows children that you care about what they think. There are many ways to do this:

- Ask about a popular show or book. What do children like or dislike about the characters or story?

- When a child shares a preference, hold onto that information and use it later so the child knows you care enough to remember. For example, "I put a strawberry on your plate because I remembered that you like strawberries," or "I remembered that you didn't like the swings at that playground, so we're going to a different one today."

- When a child reacts negatively to an activity, item, or experience, ask questions so you can understand the reaction. Keep that information in mind for future interactions.

Let Children Make Decisions

Try to give children a couple choices whenever possible. Some children may not care what dishes they eat off of or what they wear, while others will care deeply. Involving children in making these decisions helps them know that they are included and that their opinions matter. Here are some ideas for incorporating choice:

- Involve children in planning meals or snacks.

- Empower children to choose a group or family activity.

- When assigning classroom responsibilities, let children volunteer for the job they prefer.

Use Active Listening

Be available and open to hearing what children have to say. Use active listening, and repeat back what you heard when children are finished speaking. Try not to impose your ideas and perceived notions for what you think children should like, want, or do. This is especially true for issues related to gender and what it means to be a child.

If a child wants to share something with you and it really isn't a good time, explain that what they have to say is so important to you that you want to be able to give your undivided attention, but you can't do that right now. Then, let the child know when you will be able to hear what they have to say (for example, in ten minutes, or after sending an email).

Pay Attention

You can gather a lot of information from observing children. Feelings might be easy to see in young children, but you can learn a lot more by watching closely. What do children like to play and who do they like to play with? What do they like to eat? Using this information in your conversations with children can help them feel safe sharing their thoughts and feelings.

By showing children that you care about what they like and don't like and that you are interested in what they have to say about everyday things, you build a trusting relationship where they feel safe coming to you when they have something important to share. Childhood is full of challenging and confusing situations, some more serious than others. When children feel respected and heard, they know that there are adults to turn to when they are in need of guidance or help.

About the Author and Illustrator

Afsaneh Moradian (she/her) has loved writing stories, poetry, and plays since childhood. After receiving her master's in education, she took her love of writing into the classroom where she began teaching children how to channel their creativity. Her passion for teaching has lasted for over fifteen years. Afsaneh now guides students and teachers (and her young daughter) in the art of writing. She lives in New York City and Oaxaca, Mexico.

Maria Bogade (she/her) is an illustrator and author with an animation background. She loves creating illustrations with a strong narrative, colorful and beautifully composed to entertain children and adults alike. Her work is internationally published and is also found on greeting cards and products such as chocolate. With her three children and spouse, she lives in a tiny village in southern Germany where fox and hare bid each other good night.

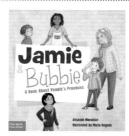

The **Jamie is Jamie series** invites young children to join Jamie as they build confidence through imaginative free play, address gender stereotypes, respect pronouns and gender identity, and learn self-advocacy skills.

More Great Books from Free Spirit

Just Because I Am
A Child's Book of Affirmation
by Lauren Murphy Payne, MSW, LCSW, illustrated by Melissa Iwai

For ages 3–8. 36 pp.; PB and HC; full-color; 11¼" x 9¼".

Zach Stands Up
by William Mulcahy, illustrated by Darren McKee

For ages 5–8. 36 pp.; HC; full-color; 8" x 8".

Free Leader's Guide
freespirit.com/leader

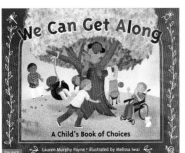

We Can Get Along
A Child's Book of Choices
by Lauren Murphy Payne, MSW, LCSW, illustrated by Melissa Iwai

For ages 3–8. 40 pp.; PB and HC; full-color; 11¼" x 9¼".

Speak Up and Get Along!
Revised & Updated Edition
by Scott Cooper
For ages 8–12. 136 pp.; PB; 2-color; illust.; 6" x 9".

I Like Being Me
Poems about kindness, friendship, and making good choices
by Judy Lalli, M.S.
For ages 4–8. 64 pp.; PB; color illust./B&W photo mix; 8" x 8".

Feel Confident!
A book about self-esteem
by Cheri J. Meiners, M.Ed., illustrated by Elizabeth Allen

For ages 4–8. 40 pp.; PB and HC; full-color; 11¼" x 9¼".

Interested in purchasing multiple quantities and receiving volume discounts?
Contact edsales@freespirit.com or call 1.800.735.7323 and ask for Education Sales.

Many Free Spirit authors are available for speaking engagements, workshops, and keynotes.
Contact speakers@freespirit.com or call 1.800.735.7323.

For pricing information, to place an order, or to request a free catalog, contact:

Free Spirit Publishing Inc.
6325 Sandburg Road • Suite 100 • Minneapolis, MN 55427-3674
toll-free 800.735.7323 • local 612.338.2068 • fax 612.337.5050
help4kids@freespirit.com • freespirit.com